THE COC SHATTERS

COLLECTION OF CONSCIOUSNESS

TRIJAL BH.

Made with ❤ on the Notion Press Platform
www.notionpress.com

In loving memory of ...

let that thought

Contents

Prologue

In case it feels for you to quit, just do it, the first few chapters are maze game, which the narrator solves quick, the science which occurs here isn't what you all expect for your life to say to you, but here it does.

Enjoy listening to it, from you to you,

Enjoy **Reader**

ONE

HI MA'AM

"Thank you everyone for your precious time." the double chinned guy aclaimed.

My legs were shivering from the stage fear where everything went monochrome. My teacher told me to calm down, I shooked my head trying to hide my voice and walked on the stage with a non working mic,
which I threw on the crowd of junior expecting a vote from each individual.
I scratched my butt and started speaking without any order, the all planning I had made, did go to waste.My 200 rupees print disappeared like Water on sun's surface. Without any hope I went to Ahane in my class hoping to get some happiness, ended up wasting my whole mood.
Ahane and I were and are good friends from 3 years, but this year was different, ofc it was my own planning of trying to date her, having a second thought she might break the good bond we shared, so I quitted, talking from maybe 4 months now, hoping one day, she might friendly ask to go out.

Suddenly I was awakened by a big earthquake, in the left side of my bed.I suddenly remembered I wasnt on my

planet or universe. here everyone and everything was different.
Even everyone called me "IDLE", then and there I quickly ran to school, where actually we were taught about the afterlife of marriage with our partner, which in this universe was the eve, my partner for current semester.
she had a pretty good face, I appreciated that, but I was always confused on how she was soo calm.Even when i broked my gym teacher's neck, when he was trying to crouch under my white pants with lasagne fallen on the left thighs.My thighs weren't that huge, but huge enough to wobble freely.
My thigh was shaking in my dream to and fro, i recalled as eve sat on my, oh sorry next to me.After the boring class of being an ideal husband for wife, I raned my way home, hoping to eat some pudding of last night.It was gone, the only thing left was a spoon covered with white fluid.
The school system which i was going through was the real issue based one, which included every small activity, but no studying as humans here believed 18 age is just a wall from reality.I was 15 and eve was 14, only for this month, her birthday is close.
Here little kids were taught of the home science knowledge and fun activites for fitness.Here children played with rabbit which were found alot here.according to science, this earth must have been finished with living as there were no carnivores, even humans were herbivores, but there was something which kept the population in check.Second day in this weired place ended by me cuddling eve on my side, where she called my name I-D-L-E each letter by letter, how it actually should be pronounced.

TWO

THE SLAUGHTER HOUSE

"Douglus!! Douglus!!"a voice in the dark waked me.

"Huh"I tooked a sigh of complete confusion.

"Where am I ?" I asked,

"Oh no! she is coming"The voice in dark said.

I tried my best to open my rusted iron cage, were suddenly an old lady came.she didn't said a word,opened the gate, and slammed me with the iron-nailed baseball bat, while her red scarf covering her hairs fell down.I waked up in the passage of a posh stairway with complete quiet, suddenly from the ceiling a bulb fell down, leaving a cracked noice,I blinked and the whole ceiling was now covered with bulbs, each ready to fall, I began to run as the bulbs loosed and the one's behind me began to fall.

A door, I shouted trying my best to run quick,the yellow bulbs began to get closer, so was I to the door,but I had white shine on my eyes, just for 2 seconds and the door was replaced with broken window covered with blood on edges.

She punched, I was back again where the old women calling me Douglus hitting me as hard as possible with the non working chainsaw,maybe it needed some oiling.

"Where is the weapon?"she shouted as she stopped the hitting and punching maybe for the search of some oil.I was hanging on some iron bar my hands tied together by two hooks which had peirced my hands which hurt alittle.

"I don't know a...any weapon." I claimed.

The old women turned back now with pink lipstick and bloodred teeths, trying her best to smile as her blooded covered hand, now covered with blue gloves ripped my white shirt.

"That was a new one, You charming." I screamed, while she starting piercing black rusted zinc nails on my stomach, trying her best to cover the blood with some cotton. After piercing about 13 nails she started to laugh and started the yellow light, shining over the walls which looked little gross.

Now completely satisfied old women packed me in a wooden box, sealed it,with one whole for breathing, I saw the day passing by the little box which I had turned completely grossed and smelly,on the 4th day I was on the verge of dying, with the pain in stomach, I punched the box with my wet hand covered with my own pu*e.I collasped, and I was woked up by a robotic voice, which when eyes opened I found myself with two black soldiers carrying me to a big and green colored algae covered river,I screamed with all I had.

"Help! Somebody, someone!"I screamed.

As I was thrown in the lake, without any sense over body, I drowned, and was unconcious.

Again I found myself in water but concious and clean, without any dirt or puke.I struggled this time with all I had.the clean water went in my throat reliefing the 4-days thirst,A hook pulled my shirt, drenching myself after a long time in pure water.

"Dry him." a raspy voice said from behind uttered.

I was thrown to a big truck this time with huge cotton bales,which absorbed my water quickly.I looked in front and found some pangles kept on a makeshift table, I ate them hurriedly, with alot of noise.

I counted my zinc nails again and started sqeezing my flat tummy and then rubbing my bald head. There wasnt any window to look through just a ceiling with lights fixed, shining brightly.

The trucked stopped,the soldier knocked the door, removed me from the truck with a gun in his hand, I followed his instructions and waited for the truck to go away.

I tooked a sigh of relief and knocking the door for the collage stood ahead of me,It was a wooden house, with beautiful lawn to look by. Knocking the door for several times, after the 19th knock, the door was opened, a women jumped, an adult one, so was I, maybe I was 27 years old.

Our lips matched and got locked for the couple for minutes which felt like seconds to me. I smiled, gaved my introduction which later followed by another kiss which got locked for the next 4 minutes.

I dont know why, but I felt this kiss familiar and walked into her house where we chit-chatted for 2 mins, I shared my weird experience and tasted the green tea which tasted soo good,I wouldnt ever forget that in the rest of my life, I though.

The tea made me drowse, I got weaker as I sipped more tea, the more I drank, the more craved for it, the more I slept by it.

THREE

THE INDEPENDENCE

"Wake up bastards, sleep is over." The manager said in a raspy voice.

"they got us cornered" I said with the other 12 women preparing for the plantation of Tea in south america. A spanish came with a whip and began to whip the women till the black turned red and then purple.I was small, not visible to them.I shouted, "mother" which made the spanish notice me, but he didnt whipped me, instead taked me to van and dropped me brutally, by holding my long hairs, which hurted abit. I with a strange face, now was in a compact room filled with 60 to 70 people pushing each other.I was barely able to move, I suddenly with a jerk fell on an uncle.

"They throwed you too from the above door. Poor girl."

I could hear gunfires from far and closed my eyes wondering about the fields I and my brother used to run before the ships had landed.

"Mother?" I shouted.

Nobody responded, maybe this was the end,I won't be able to be back to daily life and would suffer in this van for years, maybe this is how my life would end.

I closed my eyes, while the teardrop flowed over my cheeks. The suffocation was too high, I wasn't able to breathe much, Maybe I would drown in 2 mins, I said to myself. The uncle pressed my nose by his mass hardly, hard enough to make me dead. I could feel it, my death, I was dead, I had my brain working but my body wasn't responding.

"I hate you"dah said, in cryish voice, I had expected a slap but I was surprise by how she acted.

"Its ok, I just wanted you to hear it, nothing more nothing less." my thin voice said, I still wasnt sure if she was able to hear what I said to her. because like most people, everyone tries to act they are listening even though not a word goes in their stomach. I thought my dream of being an educator would never be finished, and the reason would be my physical chracteristics which I wasnt comfortable with. the bell rang, It was time to...

time for another period, But i still had the anxiety which soon fell apart as I sat attending my maths classes which I was a master at that time.With a grin and no extra thoughts in my mind, i began packng up to go home, dah didnt talked the moments, I looked a bit for her, but ended going home alone. I was happy this moment now, Because I didnt had to brainstrom anymore. With an anger on my forehead which I acquired without any reason, was removed when I punched a stranger whom I saw on the road.

Now completely unsatisfied me, reached home,washed my face on the mirror of which I was always scared of due to some reasons, changed and soon went to sleep, it was 6PM and I still had the thing going in my mind.

remembering the points, I wrote them and slept. The morning I was IDLE and the series of weird experiences begin, maybe it was my own imagination to keep me away from reality, my own subconsiousness which kept me happy or just trying to do so.

I tooked a sign of relief. "A fly went in my eye" I shouted. it hurted alot.I ran to basin and rinced it clean.My face now cover with water. I tooked my towel and started rubbing it off, the towel now covered with blood and I only able to use my left eye made the feeling too weird and painful. I drowned. The next moment Dah was next to me crying, " who told you to jump infront of car? you idiot!"

"a car? " I asked in a clumsy voice."do I have both my eyeballs?"

"yes they are, you worried about your eyeballs! " Dah exclaimed. "look at your legs, they arent even one thing yet. "

Lying on the bed, breeze coming in and out with curtains tapping the window gently I was sitting there dah on my side, not really acting like worried, asked if she might do his assignments for the period of time.

I couldnt say no, who else would do? I thought.

The breeze of the cold morning in the chilly ward, with the warm blanket. This feeling, this moment, this place felt really good, I really myself wasn't sure of what had happened to me.The thought of IDLE soon fade out, I was back to being the plane old me in my real world with dah, who literally just dumped me. I agreed of it, with abit of pain in fractured leg, I tried to move just abit to make by back feel more comforting.

Shit talks aside, I thought.Lets just sleep before its too late.I began to feel drowsy, then a deep sleep entered my face, slowly flowing down to my knees where it finally spread to whole body.

FOUR

THE END

It was midnight, the ward felt chilly, I had slept alot in noon, that I couldn't sleep at night. I felt a chill in sudden running down my neck, soon to the back of my nape. It felt as if some man in seven feet is roaming in corridor with a huge blade, mask of threaded holes.

After thinking of this weird imagination, I thought of calling Ahane, to my surprise, she was asleep.

"Its 12 at midnight, she wont alive." I thought and began to understand my own stupidity.What was I thinking when I ran in front of the car, What thought was it that made me go crazy, or was it just myself of staying crazy. whatsoever the reason might be, I just wished that I wouldn't have made things look pathetic. I hate the feeling of sympathy, I thought.

And began to close my eyes as the wind and blanket began to comfort me more.

"wake up" I really wish it is Ahane, thank god it was Ahane, that was the first time I felt happiness after waking up. I waited there for maybe a week or so.Then the craziness of the sleepdreams of that IDLE or of that woman or me being a slave in some old century, this all stopped.My brain began to feel relaxed, but..

It wasnt the end, I didnt expected my life to turned this shitty from this moment ahead, I might say crazy things in this book, the diary of a pshyco-path/logist.

FIVE

THEY WEREN'T GLIMPSES

I began dotting the points as the days of hospital were over, I was back to school, attending my regular classes. I was bored, felt all of the people to vanish but they didn't. Ahane wasn't present today, making the day more boring.

Finally the period ended, but I had to face another one, so to kill time, I went away of class for some freash air.I entered the class to find myself alone, what was going on, I wondered ?

"Access granted" a weird voice whispered in my ear.It completely felt like something was up, was there any bigger project I was part of was, I wondered.

"Maybe my school is a secret hideout for agent or maybe there's disease that makes the person disappear." thinking of this I was home, there too I couln't find anyone.It felt amazing for some time and I wondered of entering a supermart.

The supermart was open, doors ready, I entered, to my surprise the reception area was smelling rotten, ignoring it, I went straight to shopping.

Eating, drinking all I could. Then I arrived near the mouth freshner area, I ate some, to a quick I heard the sound of monkey, might be. I found the voice coming near the fish and steaks centre.

Expecting a normal monkey, I arrived there, to my surprise, it was a doll, a monkey doll, teeth ready to pierce skin, looking at me shouting with all might he could, he ranned over me, even threw a fish on me, might be salmon. It ran, so did I, I was ahead it was back, I ran quickly to the nearest restroom, entered in it, closed the goddamn door, sat on the toilet.

Hands on ears, eyes closed wishing to return everything back to normal.

"Aaaaaaaaaa!!!!!" a girl shouted with all her might," a boy in girl's restroom."

This was the very moment I wanted to get eaten by the doll, rather than getting humialiated for trespassing. I was back to the same old world, what had happened, I wondered, did I just unlocked an access to this world.

Was this world, probably could be...A simulation!

SIX

I-LASHBACK

She looked soo beautiful as I gazed in her eyes.

"Play the song", she said. I played the song as the incharge of software department. I gazed at her, and still had flashbacks about her eyes.

This was an hour ago, the feast was now over. I was wandering alone as I always used to, and expecting anything from anyone, and started my walk to my home. Strange, as it may hear, I had forgotten my house address, the only place I subconciously wanted to go, was the beach.

The waves felt like they were calling me.That was the last time, anyone saw me as myself as I vanished from the horizon. I disappeared for them, for me I was absorbed in the art of setting sun, I watched it vanishing till the bottom, standing waiting for it to go away.

What was I forgetting, did I forgot any book in school, I wondered, but it wasnt the case.

Out of the blue, I went into the blue, not the sky, the shallow sea, I felt not a drop on my body. But I felt falling deeper and deeper, I tried to wiggle my hands, but no help, I was still falling, concious for a moment, not the other.

"The sand is salty", I exclaimed. I stood up, dusted my navy blue uniform, and gazed at the blue ball which for some reason appeared like cortana.

"Where am I ?" I shouted at the blue ball.

The ball didn't speak, but answered my question, I just somehow suddenly understood that I was in my own head.

"Part of me is you now." The ball telepathy me.

"Who are you ?" I asked.

"They call me, the COC (collection of conciousness), this conciousness is really necessary for everyone, where my role come to action, Im the collection of everyones' every possible and impossible thought." Ball like thing turned air." I don't have any physical body of mine, I jsut exist and now you had have access to me, You have obtained some kind of priority which I had to clear, were you having flashbacks of people that never existed in the first place. You were peoples imagination, you were an ideal husband even at this age, an ideal meal for siberian tigers, an ideal kisser, even an ideal slave. You were peoples' desire."

Finally it all maked sense, I thought, wondered why I had that priority which he owned.

"My pronouns are'nt he, it is it, don't forget it, I may forget too if that happened", the ball telepathy.

"Why the hell I always find you in the hospital, what has gotten into you!" Ahane said with all her strength.

"What had happened?" I asked Ahane.

"You were found lying on beach, wet."

"It was true"

"You had a fever of 105.7°"

"I feel my body numb."

"What were you thinking?"

"I was just..." I was interupted by tongue which itself stuttered, I could hear my brain saying to me, 'don't tell to her.'

"How come you know I am here?"

"I was just passing by, got to heard about you, thought of having a visit."

"Isn't it funny, I always meet you in hospital."

"It is'nt funny, watch your tongue, you can't move, I can, and you are on 3rd floor, so stay careful of what you talk."

"Yes maam, I understood." I said, with a smirk on my face, wasn't ready to face the death.

SEVEN

WHY I LOVE THE BOOKS!

I began to write as I knew, staying concious will allow the COC to read mine, so to hide it, I began to write a book, but I hadn't decided the title. With a big yawn, I called it the day and got to bed.

Morning came, I woke was surprised that I woke just normal, no trouble, no hospital, no stupid beaches, just the normal room.

I opened the door, went downstairs, my 9 year old sister waiting for me, bread ready with jam rubbed professionally.

"You sleep alot." she said.

"Sorry", head confused, scratching the back of head, " it was just a bad nightmare."

"No it wasn't a nightmare."

"Shut up!"

"Brother, I didn't said a thing."

"Sorry, it wasn't for you, my inner self."

"you are my inner self." the COC felt like he wouldn't leave me.

"My pronouns are it, not he!!" COC said angrily.

I breathe out, and jumped on the.."ah, brother..."

"What happened, the chair won't break, it isn't that old." I interupted.

"Its being 5 years dad had brought those chairs, and now you can't afford anymore chairs, dad didn't save for our whole life, just enough for us to survive 2 years, and done."

"I will get a job, believe me."I said confidently, and went to attend my school, commanding her to close the door and lock carefully.

"Hi Dah, how are you?"

"I'm fine, just my hands hurt."

"why?"

"Its because of you!"

"What did I did?"

"Who keeps these many books incomplete,aren't you worried."

"Its just..."

"Stop making excuses, lets go, school will start soon."

"Yes, she is right."

"Get the hell of my brain."

"I'm in everyone's brain, its just you who can differentiate between their thoughts and mine."

"Who are you talking with?"

"Nothing, just making time table."

"You are good in lying."

"Thank you."

"you are welcome, but next time, I won't help you complete your notes."

"I didn't said to you."

"Thats rude."Dah exclaimed.

"I mean, I said thank you to you, it was just self talking, to be in discipline."I said.

"Thank god, the situation is in control, I said to myself, that dah can't hear me clearly.

Then I reached school, ready for studying, ready to get a new score. I was a bright student, ranked high in country.

Opened my book to find out that every page was covered with something written in something with pencil, each page just had 1 alphabet, written angrily, with hate, with anxiety. I didn't knew who did it. Keeping it aside, I began to try my best to focus.

Woke 2 hours later, the lecture was over, I was ready to run home, I felt the day was over, it wasn't.

Reached home, got fresh, and soon began talking to COC, but I couldn't hear him, that very moment I noted the time 12.34 PM and started my ritual of eating chips and watching television.

"I have deduced that female protaginist will die saving the male" the COC said.

"where were you?"

"Bath tub, getting cool."

I started thinking of time table and started to note the current time and soon began to study, I knew if I didn't Im for done this year, and I can't afford the next, I need to get a scholarship.

"Looks like someone is gotten into studies, poor you."

"Shut up!"

"Stop me if you."

"Oh, you challenging me."

I switched my PC and started to watch some cute cat videos, they looked very adorable to me, but maybe COC is allergic to them.

"Anything but the cats." it begged for mercy.

"Promise you'll shut up, then I might think."

"There are currently 4 thousand people watching the cat videos, I really don't care about them, but you own a small section of mine, you can't affect that with such adversity, I can't let them get into me. They make you weak from inside, then the outside and soon you are consumed totally."

"They are cats, not extraterrestrial creatures."

"think twice."

"you think thrice."

"You shut up, or I'll play it again."

"Ok"

"Say, the bathtub wash you had, why do you need it."

"I'm the COC and it literally contains all data, useful or waste, I can't judge, I'm just made from it. But you can, lucky human."

"I would rather call you lucky, everyone have their advantages, all may use it for their benefit or not use it atall." I said firmly.

"Don't you dare play philosophy with me, I have acknowledgement of every person's thinking methodolgy from past 12 years, your appears no different to me, jsut the same calm self."

"Thats what I'm, simple, calm minded and intelligent."

"No you aren't, I can see you aren't even in top 17 intelligent people alive."

"It means I'm the 18th", I said, crossing my eye towards it in my own creativity.

"You got me."

"Now shut up."

EIGHT

THE COC SHATTERS

"Say, COC, when I was living those stupidous life,what was happending in my real life ?" I asked.

It didn't respond, I noted the time, 9.00PM, and went straight to bed.

"Hey, wake up, aren't you late."COC said."Its 6AM"

"Where were you ? when did you return ?"

"Bathtub, at 5 AM."

"Brother, Ahane is waiting outside, get up, I'll send her in."

"Wait, atleast let me wear my pants."

In the end, Ahane caught me half naked.But just for like few milliseconds, but I know she won't think wrong it, not because I trust her, but because I too have got some powers, just one though, I could read the person's thought but only of Ahane in front me, very deeply.

"Enjoy it for the moment you have yourself and the power."

"I have downloaded 50 cute cat videos just for you, you ready."

"Wow, I didn't knew you were also in cats." Ahane said, surprised.

Then I would like to jump alittle ahead bacause it feels lumpy, lets get to the end.

From a month, I had noticed all patterns of COC, and it clearly is here to destroy me completely, this was done by few deduction I did many time. I had also noticed its pattern of not staying on.

According to me, COC is just a very filled collection, it really isn't any collection of world's conciousness, but it is a collection of few, it appears to be of a particular region, but I also think, that I can destroy him, if only I knew where it really is.

From details from few neighbours at the time COC is inactive, I found that I was missing for 4 days and was found to a girl named Ahane.

I just have to find where I was placed for 4 days, and thats it, I would get the exact location of COC.

This plan is full proof and I'm damn sure, it would succeed, though its risk level beign high.

At evening 6PM, COC will get inactive and that would be my chance to strike, if you found it escalated to quick, I would say, this book is written by me, notes about COC weren't written here, so all observation was contained within those pages of which I would never ever think in my time with COC.

I thought that I was kidnapped for 4 days in the warehouse which was 2km away.

I got ready at 6PM exact, and got into run, at 6.15PM I was there, clean and running, entered it, found nothing,just my socks.

It felt suspecious for me, but I could find any other clue, the only thing I was able to found or can be seen was unburned candle, I thought, maybe a secret door would open of burning it.

I tooked my whole eternity making fire for candle, but nothibng happened, frustated I threw the candle away. I was surprised to see a simple plug, bottom of the candle, pushing it opened a door, where secrets of scince were hidden. Nah, just kidding, the only thing that came was a rusted life.

The reason for why I had suspected this warehouse was du to it having a large tower just behind it.

"How long will this lift take!!" I said frustated.

After 12 mins, I was finally able to reach the ground of a posh neat centre which appeared to me as a animal husbandry for experiments. Scientist of white clothes could be seen, but no one spotted me, for few minutes, I was surprised and confused of what it was practicing here was illegal.

"Throw those brains of monkeys quickly, get rid of it.""Hey who are you, how did you came here?"

"I'm the COC", I said firmly, waiting for the coated man to respond.

"You.. are..COC" the man said laughing with all his might.

"No, my boy,I'm the real COC,you are just a part of me." "Come, I'll show you, and there he went explaining every component of this massive lab, It was impressive.

"Here at neurathink, we create reality, you are one of our first superhuman generation third. The first generation will be available to us, and then..."

"You will kidnap me again."

"Yeah, the regular sequence."

Soon he took me to the soo called gigaconsciousness web, where every possibility of a very complex event could be calculated in few seconds, where normal computers take millions of years to solve it."

"This is the COC-2 project lab, here you can see, who is control under the COC."

"I need water", I asked thirstily, for which the man agreed and gave, I drank the whole, it felt mineral fresh.

"Where is my project lab ?"I asked.

"Just aside this, COC-3 project lab, the most highly advanced with farthest connectivity."

Pointing towards a small white pearl like spinning material, he said, "this is your processor."

"Can I look closely ?" I asked innocently.

Closer I went, and soon threw all the water in my mouth on the white spinning ball, it appeared to accelerate tremendous quickly.

"What have you done, disrupted this matter with regular matter could cause a huge amount of trouble."

His words appeared to me as mere blutterings and soon I fainted.

"Wake up, I-D-L-E, drop the children to school, I'll take care of Amelia, till the moment." eve ordered.

9 798889 514992

Printed by Libri Plureos GmbH in Hamburg,
Germany